UEST FOR THE MAGIC CRYSTAL

A THUNDERCATS™ Adventure

By Cathy West

**Adapted from the teleplay
by Peter Lawrence**

Illustrated by Amador

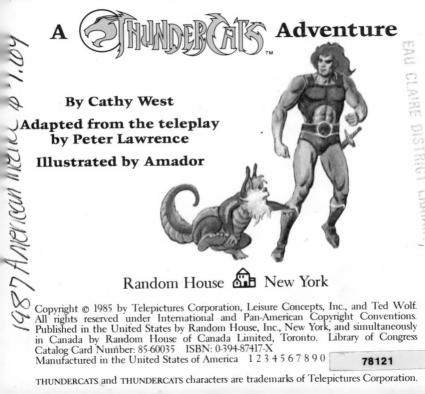

Random House New York

It was a beautiful day on Third Earth, but Lion-O, young hereditary Lord of the Thundercats, was not happy. He sat alone at the top of a mountain, dreaming of another world.

He didn't really *dislike* Third Earth. It was a wonderful planet, filled with delightful and mysterious places to explore.

But Lion-O was homesick for his *true* home—the planet Thundera—which he knew he would never, ever see again.

Lion-O had been very small when the Thundercats fled their doomed planet. He could remember looking back, horrified, as Thundera exploded into fiery fragments that twinkled like tiny fireflies against the darkness of space. But he yearned to remember more.

Lion-O jabbed at the air with the Sword of Omens, which Jaga, the wise elder, had given him when they fled. "It holds the Eye of Thundera," Jaga had said. "The source of all the Thundercats' power."

Jaga had given his life to save the Thundercats. But sometimes, just when Lion-O needed him most, a magical thing happened—Jaga appeared to him, in spirit, there on Third Earth.

"I wish Jaga were here now," said Lion-O.

"You seem troubled," said a deep voice.

Lion-O turned—it was a vision of Jaga!

"I miss Thundera," said Lion-O. "How I wish I could learn more about it!"

Jaga smiled. "There is a way I can show it to you."

"How?" said Lion-O.

"When we left Thundera, we brought with us an Optocrystal—a time capsule," said Jaga. "It contained the history of our planet. Find it, Lion-O, and you will learn all about your childhood—and much more."

"Jaga—" cried Lion-O.

But the vision was gone.

Lion-O raced back to the Cats' Lair, the Thundercats' mighty fortress. Nearly everyone was there: Tygra, master of camouflage; Cheetara, the swift one; Panthro, martial arts expert; and the mischievous Wilykit and Wilykat. Snarf, who had looked after Lion-O on Thundera, was taking his afternoon nap.

Breathless, Lion-O told them of the Optocrystal.

"Amazing!" said Tygra. "I thought it was destroyed when we crashed to Third Earth."

"How can we find it?" Lion-O asked eagerly.

Panthro drew a crude map. "We must make a thorough search of the area. Get Snarf, Lion-O, and we'll each take a different direction."

Within minutes they were off.

"Can't we stop and take a break?" whined Snarf a little later as he and Lion-O hiked through the Forest of the Unicorns.

"In a minute," said Lion-O.

Soon they came to the River of Despair. Its slimy purple and green waters gurgled sluggishly in the sunlight.

"Ooohh, dear!" moaned Snarf. "How will we ever get across *that*?"

Lion-O laughed. "What's the matter, Snarf? Can't you swim?" And to Snarf's dismay, the young lord began to wade into the murky waters.

Suddenly the river seemed to explode!

Up reared a horrible Black Widow Shark! She chomped her vicious jaws and roared with rage as Lion-O leaped back to the safety of the riverbank just in time.

"You are very lucky, my young friend," a high, sweet voice sang out from the woods. Out stepped the white-haired Unicorn Keeper with a beautiful unicorn at her side.

"The Black Widow Shark," the old woman continued, "lies in wait for anyone who tries to cross the River of Despair."

"Then how will we ever get to the other side?" asked Lion-O.

The Unicorn Keeper smiled. "I know a way."

The Unicorn Keeper waved her hand and several unicorns came out of the forest, each carrying a glittering diamond in its mouth. When they piled the jewels on the riverbank, a beam of light rose up and formed a bridge over the River of Despair.

"Be quick, now!" urged the Unicorn Keeper. "The power will not last long!"

"Thank you!" Lion-O called as he and Snarf hurried safely over the bridge to the other side. Now they could continue their quest for the Optocrystal.

But elsewhere another Thundercat had dug up a few problems of his own!

"Burrow... burrow... burrow..." A scraggly line of Molemen chanted in weary unison as they tramped, heads down, through a dark tunnel.

"Uh, excuse me," said Tygra, materializing from the walls. "Have any of you guys seen an Optocrystal? It's a kind of box..."

"Burrow... burrow... burrow..." The workers trudged on, blind to Tygra's presence.

Suddenly the Molemaster charged in, gleefully cracking his thick, metal-spiked whip.

"You lazy Molemen!" he bellowed. "You must work harder! Dig more gold!" Then he spotted Tygra.

"What's this? A *trespasser* in the Mines of the Molemen?" he cried. "You'll pay for this!" He cracked his whip, but it struck bare wall—Tygra had disappeared!

"Behind you, wart!" shouted Tygra, laughing. Then he lashed out with his own whip. The tip struck the ground, shooting sparks that singed the Molemaster's hairy hands. The evil slave driver fled in terror.

"*Now* will you help me?" Tygra asked the Molemen.

"Burrow... burrow... burrow..." The downtrodden workers seemed not to hear.

Tygra shook his head. "I don't think they'd see the Optocrystal if it was right in front of their noses!"

Not far away, Cheetara had stopped by the edge of a swamp to rest.

"How lovely!" she said, bending to look at some multicolored water lilies. Then she froze. Something had hissed behind her.

She whirled around. A giant serpent struck with lightning speed, but Cheetara, even faster, blocked its lethal blow with her magic staff.

"Well, well," said Cheetara. "Let's see how fast you *really* are!" She began to run dizzying circles around the serpent. It struck, struck, struck at the air—and finally sank its fangs into its own tail!

"Heads I win . . . tails you lose!" said Cheetara, laughing, as she sped away.

Meanwhile, Panthro had stopped to explore a strange rocky beach.

"Hmmm, no sign of the Optocrystal here," he said. But as he turned to go, he came face to face with a seven-foot-tall Crabman whose tiny eyes stuck out on thin stalks. With an eerie cry, the creature attacked Panthro with viselike pincers.

"Now you've done it . . . you've gone and made me mad!" said Panthro. "In fact, I feel downright *crabby*!" And with a high-flying kick, he sent the Crabman tumbling through the air.

By now Lion-O and Snarf's search had brought them to the top of a steep mountain. Below, at the mouth of a dark cave, something glinted in the sunlight.

Quickly Lion-O raised his sword in the air. "Mighty Sword of Omens," he cried, "give me *sight beyond sight*!" Immediately the Sword's crossbar curled, forming eyeholes. As Lion-O gazed through them, he saw a large, glittering object—bearing the proud symbol of the Thundercats!

"Snarf! It must be the Optocrystal!" cried Lion-O. "Time to call the others!"

Lion-O stood tall on the mountaintop and raised the Sword of Omens to the heavens.

"Thunder-Thunder-Thunder-Thundercats—Ho!" he cried. Immediately the Sword began to glow and then grew to three times its length. The Eye of Thundera snapped open with a mighty roar and flashed the bold Thundercats symbol into the sky. The other Thundercats—wherever on Third Earth they might be—would see this signal and would soon be at Lion-O's side.

But Lion-O couldn't wait. Cautiously he and Snarf crept to the mouth of the cave.

Suddenly Snarf shrieked. A huge, ugly caveman had emerged from the darkness.

"Pardon me," said Lion-O. "But this Optocrystal belongs to us. So, if you don't mind, we'll just—"

"Rrraahhrrgghh!" cried the caveman. He sank to his knees and propped his elbow on the shining silver object.

"Hey! I think he wants me to arm-wrestle for it!" exclaimed Lion-O.

"Oh, no!" groaned Snarf. "He's too big! You'll never be able to beat him!"

By the time the other Thundercats had raced into the clearing, Lion-O and the caveman were locked in a contest of pure strength, their arm muscles rippling with effort. Finally, with a roar, Lion-O slammed the caveman's fist down onto the surface of the Optocrystal.

"He did it!" Wilykit and Wilykat shouted at once, dancing around the clearing.

The caveman grunted and disappeared into the cave.

"Now," said Lion-O, "let's take this Optocrystal home—where it belongs!"

Back at the Cats' Lair, Lion-O watched the Optocrystal's flashing images again and again. Tears came to his eyes. Thundera had been so wonderful; he could hardly believe it was really gone.

Finally Lion-O turned away. Thundera would always be a part of him. Now it was time to make Third Earth his new home.